TALES OF THE INSECT SURGERY

W. G. Mead

ARTHUR H. STOCKWELL LTD
Torrs Park, Ilfracombe, Devon, EX34 8BA
Established 1898
www.ahstockwell.co.uk

British Library Cataloguing-in-Publication Data.
A catalogue record for this book is available
from the British Library.

ISBN 978-0-7223-4924-3
Printed in Great Britain by
Arthur H. Stockwell Ltd
Torrs Park   Ilfracombe
Devon EX34 8BA

CONTENTS

THE SURGERY

There is a doctor's surgery for people; there is a veterinary surgery for animals.

Did you know that there is an insect surgery for all the insects and creatures like snails, slugs, worms, and even a few bigger ones like slow-worms and tiny frogs?

The surgery is managed by a Dr Earwig and his very able and hard-working assistant, Nurse Ant. Dr Earwig is quite a happy earwig, larger than most; but for all that, he is always there to help any insect that is in trouble, no matter where they are – Nurse Ant will follow the Doctor no matter how far it might be. Gardens are very big places for small insects and they cannot always get to the surgery themselves.

The Doctor and Nurse Ant make all their own medicines from the fruit and flowers in the garden and with a supply of honey from the bees. Nurse Ant is very clever at making bandages from grass and preparing leaves for beds for the stay-over patients.

They both enjoy their work, getting all the unwell insects and other creatures well, and those that have had accidents better. Nothing is too much trouble for them.

The surgery is halfway down Blossom Avenue in a large back garden. In the middle of the garden is a very tall silver birch tree, so tall that it reaches above the rooftops. At the bottom of the garden is an old apple tree, next to which is a garden shed. Now, at the bottom of the shed there are two bricks holding up the corner. The space between the bricks, you will notice, is a well-worn path leading into a large area under the shed. You will also see smaller areas on either side of a passage that runs along a little way. These small areas along the passage are for stay-over patients, so they have little grass beds in them. In the centre of the big space is a flat stone with a fresh leaf on it. This is where Dr Earwig examines his patients. All around are medicines and ointments neatly stacked because Nurse Ant will not have it any other way but neat.

"It's easier to find things in a hurry," she says.

By the entrance on a small, flat stone is an emergency bag, always ready-packed in case Dr Earwig and Nurse Ant have to rush off and help some insect that is ill or has had an accident.

Any insect from anywhere can attend the surgery – no insect or other garden creature will be turned away.

Every insect knows how to find the surgery. All they need to do is to look up and find the tall silver birch tree. Once they are in the garden, any insect living there will tell them the way.

Now, I would like to tell you about some of the illnesses and accidents which Dr Earwig and Nurse Ant have had to deal with.

THE FALLEN SPIDER

One day Nurse Ant had just returned from collecting nectar to make her special nectar juice when two spiders arrived, bringing with them their friend. Apparently, they had all been playing a game of dare on the cobweb to see who could drop down their threads the fastest.

Unfortunately one of the threads had broken quite high above the ground and the spider had fallen very hard on to the ground. He was now feeling very dizzy and out of breath, and he was very worried about the spinneret on the lower part of his body, because this spins his web and, of course, without it the little spider couldn't do any spinning.

Dr Earwig laid him down on a large, flat stone covered with a clean, fresh leaf. It was Nurse Ant's duty to change the leaves regularly to keep the surgery fresh and clean. Dr Earwig examined all the spider's eyes for damage, but he could not find any sign of injury. They were all bright and shiny – no problem there. Then he used a rolled-up blade of grass to listen to the spider's chest. That was slightly dusty and a little bruised, but there was nothing to

worry about. After this he looked at the spider's spinneret. He asked the Nurse to bathe it with nectar juice to clean it to stop any germs getting in.

While all this was happening the spider's two friends were waiting nervously outside, hoping that all was well with their injured friend.

After a very close examination, Dr Earwig said to the spider, "The dizziness will go. You are out of breath because you hit your chest badly, but this should ease up quickly."

To make sure that the spider was healthy he asked him to crawl up the wall and hang from the ceiling. This was to test his spinneret and web thread to make sure they were in perfect working order.

So very carefully the spider walked up the wall, out on to the ceiling, and there he fastened his thread firmly. Then, with his eyes tightly closed and a little fearful of falling again, he let go with all his legs at once. He dropped suddenly, coming to a quick stop on the end of his thread with a slight jerk.

After a second or so he opened his eyes, looked to make sure he was safe and shouted at the top of his voice, "YES!"

At that moment both of his friends came rushing in to see him dangling safely on his thread, none the worse for his accident.

"Can he go home now?" they asked.

"Yes," said Dr Earwig. But, with a wink to Nurse Ant, he gave them a stern warning not to be so silly again. He then turned to Nurse Ant and said, "Spiders will be spiders."

MRS MILLIPEDE'S LEGS

After doing a house call to a family of greenfly who lived in an old rose bush at the back end of the garden, Dr Earwig felt sure he would have to visit them again soon as two of the youngest ones had got black spot from eating some bad rose leaves.

Dr Earwig entered the surgery between the two bricks under the shed and was immediately told by Nurse Ant that Mrs Millipede, who lived under the woodpile, was waiting in the surgery suffering from bad legs. She had been out gathering food for all her family when the wind had blown a heavy stick off the woodpile on to her legs. Somehow she had managed to limp her way to the surgery, but two of her legs were broken and another three were badly sprained and bruised.

Dr Earwig went in to see her straight away and found her very jolly under the circumstances.

"What on earth have you been doing?" he asked.

After she explained everything again to the Doctor, she added, "It's a good job I've another hundred pairs of legs."

And they both had a good laugh.

"Well, how are you going to mend them?" Mrs Millipede enquired.

"First of all I must send Nurse to collect some beeswax from the hive in the apple tree. The bees are very good – they keep me supplied when I need it. Then I shall use it to make casts for your legs," the Doctor explained.

After sending Nurse Ant off to collect the beeswax, Dr Earwig started to treat the damaged legs. First he cleaned them with nectar juice, then he wound some very fine cobweb silk round them to prevent the beeswax from sticking to Mrs Millipede's legs, because when the beeswax had dried it would act like a plaster cast and set firm, keeping the legs in place while they healed.

The Doctor had only just finished attending to Mrs Millipede when Nurse Ant walked into the surgery. She told the Doctor that a worker bee would be bringing the beeswax because if it was not brought to the surgery quickly it would set, and they could not use it.

Sure enough, two minutes later there was a buzzing at the entrance to the surgery.

"Here you are, Doctor: two bags of beeswax as ordered. It's lovely and fresh and won't take long to set," said the bee.

She quickly undid the two bags attached to either leg and handed them to the waiting doctor.

"I'll be off now. Cheerio!"

And the bee flew out of the door.

"Goodbye, and thanks," the Doctor shouted after him, but the bee was already out of the entrance and on his way back to the hive.

Quickly, with the help of Nurse Ant, Dr Earwig spread the beeswax all over the broken legs.

"Well, that's nice and warm," Mrs Millipede told them.

"Try not to move your legs; otherwise they won't set right and your legs may not heal properly," warned Nurse Ant.

When the waxing was finished they got Mrs Millipede into a tiny seedling pot, which had rolled under the shed a long time ago. It was now scrubbed clean and lined with nice fresh grass cuttings, and here she waited patiently while the wax hardened.

After a while Dr Earwig checked to see that the wax had set hard.

"That looks fine. Are you ready to go?" the Doctor asked.

"Yes, I'm ready," Mrs Millipede replied as she wobbled, trying to stand on all her other legs.

"I'll see you in a few days' time to take the wax off," Nurse Ant told her.

Without more ado, Mrs Millipede waddled out of the surgery, lurching from side to side.

All the Doctor and Nurse Ant could do was to hold their sides laughing – Mrs Millipede looked so funny!

THE WORM'S TAIL

It was a warm, sunny day in the garden. Everything was peaceful – that was until the owner of the garden decided to cut the lawn. As soon as the lawnmower started up, Dr Earwig knew there would be plenty of minor injuries to the insects.

"Get lots of rose ointment and nectar ear drops ready. I think it's going to get busy later," shouted Dr Earwig to Nurse Ant above the noise of the lawnmower.

He was right, of course, and a short while later, after the lawnmower had stopped, the casualties started to drift into the surgery. In a mad rush to get down their tunnels, out of the way of the lawnmower, there were ants by the dozen with bruised and scuffed knees, a sore head or two and plenty of banged elbows. Greenfly, of course, having very sensitive ears, were a very different case. They suffered with aching ears from the noise, and so the queue to see the Doctor grew longer and longer.

"Nurse Ant, greenfly first – a touch of nectar juice in each ear and they will be fine, but go gently. Ants next – I think a little rose-petal ointment on elbows and knees should do it. And don't worry about their heads too much as they are as thick as an acorn shell." The Doctor instructed Nurse Ant what to do.

A few earwigs entered the surgery with scraped backs as they had not moved quickly enough out of the way of the lawnmower when the cutters started going. Nurse Ant knew just what to do here: a fine covering of beeswax and they would soon be better. Once she had finished, the earwigs were allowed to go home.

Unfortunately, there is always one bad accident on days like this, and sure enough in through the opening to the surgery struggled a little worm who was very upset indeed.

"Can you help me, please, Dr Earwig? A part of my tail has been cut off by the lawnmower, and it stings," sobbed the tearful chubby little worm.

"Wow, that does look bad! But never mind – we will soon see to that and in a little while it should grow back as good as new. Can you manage to get on to the leaf on the stone slab?" asked the Doctor.

"I'm sure I can," answered the chubby little worm, and he crawled carefully up on to the leaf and settled down with his tail pointing towards the door.

Nurse Ant carefully pulled some bits of gravel and grass from the wound in his tail.

"Does that hurt?" the Nurse asked.

"No, not very much," the little worm replied, trying to be very brave.

"That's good news," said the Doctor.

After the Nurse had given the wound a good clean (as it was very dirty), she asked Dr Earwig how they should treat it. The Doctor was quiet for a moment, thinking of the best way to treat the little worm.

"I think we will apply a honey poultice – that's the best thing to heal it quickly – but I'm afraid you will have to spend at least another day with us in the earth pit to make sure it heals well."

Now, the earth pit was further under the shed and was a lovely cool, damp place just for sick worms. It was near enough for the Doctor to keep a close eye on his patients while they got better.

"That's OK. It means I can put my tail up and have a nice rest. Ouch – that hurts!" he cried as his tail wiggled to his laughter.

"Do keep still," Nurse Ant said sharply as she mixed some very thin blades of grass into the honey to form a big poultice.

The Nurse then started to put the poultice on to the end of his tail, where it was cut off.

"To make sure it won't move I will put some cobweb silk over it and that will keep it on. How's that?" she asked the worm.

"It's a little bit sticky, but not too bad," replied the worm.

"Right then, all we have to do now is to get down into the earth pit and you can relax. By the way, how did you manage to lose a piece of your tail?" she asked.

"Well, I was nearly all the way down my hole, with just my tail poking out, when the lawnmower caught me," explained the little worm.

"Ouch!" said Dr Earwig, and both he and Nurse Ant cringed at the thought.

"How are we going to get the worm into the pit?" asked the Nurse.

"Easy," replied the Doctor with a hint of a smile, and then he started to lay out lots of twigs all the way to the earth pit. When this was done he said, "Now all we have to do is to roll the little worm along the logs."

As they pulled him along the logs, the logs rolled as he went over them, just like wheels. He came right to the edge of the earth pit, then with one big tug the little worm slid safely into the pit.

'My, my, I'm going to enjoy my stay here,' thought the little worm as he slid into the earth.

"I think after all this you had better learn to move faster down holes," laughed Nurse Ant, and Dr Earwig agreed.

"Next patient, please," said the Doctor as he and the Nurse left the little worm cosy and asleep in the cool, damp earth pit.

MR EARWIG'S MISHAP

It was late afternoon and nearly time for Dr Earwig to have his usual short nap. Having an afternoon doze, he found, helped him to keep going until late in the evening.

Just as he had settled down he heard a noise at the front entrance of the surgery. Straight away he went to find out what it was, and he saw coming towards him a very bedraggled earwig, soaking wet and with grazes on his body, looking as though he had been pulled through a hedge backwards.

"My, my, what have we got here? You do look a mess! Let's get you on to the stone slab so I can have a look at your injuries. I think we had better dry you first."

The Doctor began rubbing him down with some very fine moss, which quickly soaked up all the water.

"Now you are dry, perhaps we can see more clearly what is wrong with you. Mainly bruises, I think, and a few scuffs. Mind you, that pincer of yours looks like it has split. I'll have to use a splint on that so it heals properly," mumbled the Doctor to nobody in particular.

Dr Earwig called for Nurse Ant to come and help him.

"Coming," she shouted back, and she appeared immediately.

"Hello – it looks like I'm going to be busy today," she said as she started rubbing some rose-petal ointment gently all over the earwig's back, getting into every graze and scuff. Finally she covered the grazes with a thin coat of beeswax.

"While you finish there, Nurse, I'll get on and make a splint for his pincer," Dr Earwig told the Nurse, and he began shaping a tiny rose thorn to fit the pincer exactly.

There wasn't too much work to do because the thorn was already nearly the shape of the pincer.

"That's all the ointment on," said Nurse Ant, wiping herself clean with some moss.

The Doctor then started to bind the splint he had made on to the pincer of the earwig with cobweb silk. This would keep it firm until the pincer healed.

"In a few days you can come back and we will take off the splint and you will be as good as new," said the Doctor.

Dr Earwig decided that it would be better if the earwig stayed there for a short while – at least until the aches and pains had gone. Around

about, under the shed, there were lots of little bits of tubing that the owner of the shed had dropped in the past while working there. These had become very useful to the Doctor. With the Nurse's help he had cleaned them and lined them with moss and grass, so now they were turned into lovely soft beds for the sick insects to recover in.

Without any rush, and very gently, the Doctor and Nurse Ant helped the earwig into the nearest tube.

"Rest there for a while and you can go home later," Nurse Ant said.

She started to tidy up the surgery while the Doctor went back to the earth pit to see how the little worm that had an accident with his tail was getting on. The Doctor checked the honey poultice at the end of his tail and it seemed to be just fine.

"I think we can take this off now," the Doctor said, and he removed the poultice.

The little worm's tail had healed beautifully and was as good as new.

"That's fine – you can go home now, but be careful as I spotted a few big thrushes in the garden earlier," warned the Doctor.

"Thank you for making my tail better, and thank you for warning me about the thrushes," said the little worm, and like a magician he disappeared into the grass.

"How is my other patient doing?" enquired the Doctor.

"All ready to go. I feel much better now," said the earwig.

"Good, but how did that happen anyway?" the Doctor and Nurse Ant asked together.

"Well, I was going up the path, just by a little pile of gravel, when – swoosh! – some water was sloshed down the path and I was tumbled over and over in the pile of gravel. It was very painful, I can tell you," he explained.

"You had better keep your eyes and ears open next time. Good luck," said the Doctor, and off went the earwig. "Nurse, please get some more rose-petal ointment as we are getting low now," Dr Earwig said. "I need to put my feet up for a minute as I have been on the move all day long, but call me if you want me, won't you?"

"I will," the Nurse replied.

THE STAG BEETLE'S HORNS

Dr Earwig was standing at the entrance to the surgery, watching the sun begin to rise. Then coming across the garden he saw a very large stag beetle. He was walking along with his head bowed and his horns rubbing along the ground. The stag beetle stopped at the surgery entrance.

"Hello, Mr Stag Beetle. You seem to be very slow today. Are you OK?" asked the Doctor.

"I seem to have a problem keeping my head up, which makes my horns drag on the ground. It's jolly hard work to walk, and if I fly I can't see where I'm going. My head keeps dropping down and I keep bumping my head," the poor stag beetle told the Doctor in one big gasp.

"Your horns look much bigger than they were last time I saw them. Have you rubbed them down lately on a rough surface?" enquired the Doctor.

"I'm afraid not because my neck has been aching and I cannot keep lifting my head to rub them down," said the sorrowful stag beetle.

"Now, don't upset yourself. We shall soon have you sorted out. What we will do, I think, is to try and take some of the horn off. It won't hurt and we will see whether it makes any difference to you. Please rest your head over on that stone," said the Doctor, pointing to the stone.

Once the Doctor saw that the stag beetle was comfortable, he started to trim the horns with his pincers – first one and then the other, just like when we trim our nails.

Sometime later, with a pile of horn clippings at his feet, the Doctor asked the stag beetle to lift his head. The stag beetle lifted his head off the stone and, to his amazement, found he was looking straight ahead, instead of looking at the ground.

"Goodness me, my head feels a lot lighter and I can see around the horns as well. No more bumping things now! How can I thank you, Doctor?" asked the stag beetle.

"That's no problem – it's all in a day's work. But you must remember to rub them down more often; otherwise you will start to have neck ache again. Also you will be bumping into things again. If your horns get too heavy the weight will pull your head down, so be warned."

"I had better be on my way now," said the stag beetle, and he made his way to the entrance.

Once outside, he took off, shaking his head and looking to the left and right to make sure he

could see properly. Then, with a quick turn, he went home.

Dr Earwig was just clearing the mess of horn clippings away when Nurse Ant came into the surgery.

"Good morning, Doctor. I wonder if we will be busy today," she said as she looked around and saw the clippings.

"Busy or not, I've done a day's work already," the Doctor answered as he picked up the last of the horn clippings.

THE BLUEBOTTLE

The day was very hot outside. Dr Earwig was feeling very weary – he had been working most of the morning with Nurse Ant, getting a few ingredients together for his medicines, which would be made later. There were fresh rose petals for ointment; nectar juice, which was very good for cleaning wounds; and dandelion leaves for his very own dandelion linctus, for coughs. He even used it himself.

Meanwhile Nurse Ant was putting fresh bedding in the little resting tubes at the back of the surgery.

A shadow darkened the entrance to the surgery, and Dr Earwig looked up to see a bluebottle at the entrance.

"Come in, come in," invited the Doctor.

"I don't live in this garden, but I was told that I could see you," said the very worried bluebottle.

"It doesn't matter where you live – we are here to help. So how can we help you?" enquired the Doctor.

"I seem to have lost my sense of smell, so I cannot find any food that is rotting and I therefore cannot eat it or lay any eggs in it," answered the bluebottle.

"Oh dear – that is a problem! Have you hit your nose or banged your head or landed heavily on something?" questioned the Doctor.

"Not that I can remember – nothing like that at all," answered the fly.

"Perhaps your nose just needs cleaning out. I have an idea," said the Doctor with a twinkle in his eye. "Nurse Ant!" shouted the Doctor.

Nurse Ant came running back to the surgery.

"What is it?" the Nurse wanted to know. She seemed to be a bit flustered.

"Calm down, Nurse. There is no need to panic."

The Doctor lowered his voice so the bluebottle could not hear and whispered a few instructions to the Nurse, who rushed out of the surgery into the garden.

"Would you please wait over there a while until the Nurse gets back?" the Doctor asked the bluebottle.

While the fly was waiting, the Doctor carried on making his nectar juice. This juice was used for a lot of cures, from bellyache to sore feet.

It was not long before Nurse Ant returned holding a small bundle – something wrapped in a leaf. She held it at arm's length and trying to hold her breath.

"Put it down there," the Doctor said.

She placed the bundle on the floor gently, so as not to disturb what was inside, then she ran quickly back to the entrance, well away from the bundle.

"Mrs Bluebottle, could you come over here, please? When I undo the bundle, I want you to take a deep breath. Right, are you ready? Now!"

With that he undid the bundle. The bluebottle took an enormous breath, but nothing appeared to happen. Then suddenly the bluebottle started to cough, splutter, and sneeze uncontrollably.

"What is that terrible smell?" gasped the bluebottle, sucking in great amounts of air.

"Whoopee! It worked!" laughed Dr Earwig.

"What worked?" the bluebottle wanted to know.

"Well, I sent Nurse Ant to the compost heap in the garden to find a piece of garlic, and it certainly cleared your nose. You should be able to smell rotten food for miles around now."

"Now, that is what I call a good idea! I'd better be on my way now. Thank you, Doctor."

The bluebottle went to the entrance and took a big breath – a very long sniff – and took off to see what goodies she could smell.

"Nurse Ant, please get rid of this bundle," the Doctor asked.

"Not this time! I still smell from bringing it in – I hate garlic," the Nurse replied quickly.

"I suppose I had better take it out myself."

So the Doctor picked up the smelly bundle, and holding it at arm's length he went back to the compost heap and left it there.

"I think I need a rest after all this activity."

So the Doctor went back to the surgery and sat down and put his feet up for a well-earned rest.

THE GROUNDED MOTH

Dr Earwig had just finished attending to the Mother and Larva Clinic when a breathless ladybird came rushing into the surgery. She was hardly able to speak she was gasping so hard.

"Whatever is the matter?" asked the Doctor with Nurse Ant peering over his shoulder.

"It's a moth – she is on the ground and doesn't seem able to fly. Oh, please hurry, Doctor!" gasped the ladybird.

"I will come right away."

The Doctor packed his first-aid kit into a leaf bag and followed the ladybird out of the surgery door, leaving Nurse Ant to look after everything. With the ladybird leading at a fast pace in order to avoid the birds in the garden, they covered the ground very quickly, scampering up the path and across the flower bed to the old rose bush. Just underneath it they found the moth looking very agitated.

"How are you doing?" asked Dr Earwig.

"Not too good, I'm afraid," replied the moth

with a little tremble in her voice.

"Now now, don't cry. Everything will be all right – you will see."

"It's my wing, Doctor – it seems very heavy and I cannot take off," sobbed the moth.

"Let me have a good look at it."

The Doctor crawled under the moth's left wing, and stuck firmly to the underside of the wing was a rose thorn.

"Well, well, what have you been up to? The reason you cannot fly is that you have a rose thorn in your wing like a splinter. It should come out quite easily and then you will be able to fly again. I don't think it will hurt you any."

Dr Earwig gave the thorn a tug, but it would not move.

Just then the ladybird called out a warning as a large thrush had settled in a nearby tree. Dr Earwig, the ladybird and the moth all froze at the same time and clever Dr Earwig managed to bend a stem of a dandelion leaf so that the leaf covered all three of them. After a few minutes looking around, the thrush flew away.

"Now let's have another go at this thorn. Mrs Ladybird, if you will pull at the same time as I do it should come out. After a count of three – one, two, three, heave!"

With that they both pulled together, and with a sudden rush the thorn came out, leaving the Doctor and Mrs Ladybird struggling to get up from under the thorn, which had fallen on them both. By the time they got up the moth was happily flapping both her wings at the same time.

"Oh, that's very good. Now just let me put a little rose-petal ointment into the wound and in a couple of hours you should feel fine," said the Doctor, reaching into his first-aid bag for the rose ointment.

"Thank you, Dr Earwig, and thank you too very much, Mrs Ladybird, for fetching the Doctor to me," said the grateful moth.

The moth flapped her wings two or three times to make sure they worked, then with one last push down the moth took off and headed straight for the cabbage patch.

"I'll go home straight from here – it will only take a moment." And off the ladybird flew.

Without a moment to lose, the Doctor ran all the way back down the path to the surgery entrance with his first-aid bag bumping on his back.

'Another satisfied customer!' he thought with a slight nod of his head.

GRANDDAD WOODLOUSE

Dr Earwig had made all his outside calls that morning. The snail twins had a cough, but with a little dandelion syrup they would soon be fine. One of the ladybird family had caught a wing as she shut her wing case after flying home, but it was only bruised so there was nothing much Dr Earwig could do there. Just a little acorn oil was needed to sooth it. He had popped in to see Mrs Millipede to check how her legs were healing.

"They could not be better," Mrs Millipede told him.

"Well, don't forget to come into the surgery in two days and get the casts taken off," the Doctor reminded her.

Now it was time for the Doctor to get back to the surgery.

"I had better make haste – it looks like rain," Dr Earwig mumbled to himself as he hurried back to the surgery between the two bricks under the shed.

There Nurse Ant greeted him with a cheery

"Hello. How was everything today?"

"Fine – just fine. Any patients waiting for me?" he enquired.

"Oh yes, Mr and Mrs Woodlouse have brought their granddad in," Nurse Ant replied.

"What is wrong with him, do you know?" asked the Doctor.

"Well, it seems that he cannot straighten up after he rolled himself into a ball. Apparently it came on quite suddenly," Nurse Ant explained.

"Hmm, I will have to give him a thorough examination."

So the Doctor asked Mr and Mrs Woodlouse to roll Granddad Woodlouse on to the stone slab so he could have a look at him. With a great effort they managed to get Granddad Woodlouse up on to the leaf-covered slab.

"Now, everybody outside, please," the Doctor ordered, then he turned to Granddad and asked him where the stiffness was.

"It's right in between my second and third shell pieces," answered Granddad Woodlouse.

Looking between the plates on the woodlouse's back, the Doctor gradually worked his way towards the second and third shell pieces.

"Ah! Here we are! I have found the trouble. It seems you have managed to get some mud wedged between the plates and it has dried and hardened so that you cannot straighten out properly," explained the Doctor.

47

"Yes, that sounds right. I rolled into some mud the other day, quite by accident," Granddad Woodlouse remembered.

"If you can manage to stay still I should be able to soak the mud with some water and then brush it out," said the Doctor.

Dr Earwig poured the water between the second and third shell pieces, which started Granddad Woodlouse giggling.

"Sorry," the woodlouse apologised.

"Never mind – it won't be long now," the Doctor told him as he busily mopped out the mud with some moss on a stick.

Once it had all gone and the shell pieces were perfectly dry the Doctor asked Granddad Woodlouse to straighten himself out to his full length, and for the first time in days he managed to do just that.

"Goodness gracious, that's much better!" the delighted woodlouse said, rolling into a ball and out again as quickly as he could.

"Now I'll just go over your hinges with a little acorn oil and you will be your old self once again," Dr Earwig told him.

After he had finished the last hinge, the Doctor called in Mr and Mrs Woodlouse to help Granddad out.

"I don't need any help now, thank you," he told them.

With that, he rolled up quickly into a ball and

straightened out again just as quickly to prove that he was fine again.

"Right, no more mudbaths!" Nurse Ant said.

"Not if I can help it," Granddad Woodlouse replied as he walked out of the surgery without any help at all.

"Bye-bye, Doctor," Mr and Mrs Woodlouse shouted in unison.

"Cheerio," Dr Earwig and Nurse Ant answered together.

Then Nurse Ant went off to make them both some lunch.

THE SNAIL'S EYE

It was midday. In the surgery Dr Earwig and Nurse Ant were having a little rest after a very busy morning. They both heard the scraping noise before they saw the big snail that had come into the surgery. He almost filled the surgery up with his large shell.

"My goodness, you are a big snail! Are you feeling unwell?" Nurse Ant asked him, stretching her neck to take a good look at the snail.

Meanwhile, the Doctor was having a look around the snail's shell to see that everything was OK, waiting for the snail to tell him what was wrong.

"So what is the trouble you are having?" asked the Doctor.

"My left eye is very sore and keeps watering, even when it goes back into its stalk," the snail explained as a big tear fell on to the floor from the sore eye.

"Nurse, can you get me something to stand on so that I can see?"

Nurse Ant quickly got a large stone, which was

tucked in the corner. She rolled it to the Doctor, who placed it just by the snail's head.

"That's better – now I can see properly. Just tilt your head forward a little. Good – that's enough."

Dr Earwig proceeded to examine the snail's sore eye. As all snails' eyes are on stalks, the Doctor had to hold the stalk down so that he could look into the eye itself.

"No wonder your eye is hurting – you have a nasty scratch on the eye. How do you think that happened?" the Doctor asked.

"I really cannot say. My eyes are well protected normally as they go back into their stalks when anything touches them," answered the snail.

"Let me put some nectar-and-honey ointment on the eye. That should soothe the soreness," said the Doctor.

While the Doctor was tending to the snail, Nurse Ant was looking at the stalk that the sore eye was on. The Nurse tapped the Doctor on the shoulder.

"What is it, Nurse?"

"I was just thinking perhaps it's not anything outside that has scratched his eye, but something in the stalk as the eye goes back in," explained the Nurse.

"My, that's a thought! I'd better have a very close look at the stalk of that eye."

The Doctor started to examine the stalk of the sore eye, and he was about halfway down the

stalk when he found a tiny piece of seed, which was wedged tightly in the skin of the snail.

"Hold on – this might hurt a little," he told the snail, and with the help of a pair of tweezers he pulled the piece of seed from the snail's eyestalk.

"Ouch – that hurt! I hope that's all of the seed, Doctor," cried the snail.

"Yes, that is all of it. We will just bathe where it came out with honey and nectar and this should stop the eye from being scratched again."

So the Doctor bathed the spot where the seed was pulled out, making sure every bit was covered.

"Now pop your eye in and out of its stalk and see whether it hurts."

The snail did what he was told to do. In and out went his eyes – both of them.

"That feels a lot better, Doctor. Thank you, Doctor, and you too, Nurse," said the snail, using his bad eye to look around to make sure it was better.

"Now you had better get home and rest the eye for a little. It will give me more room in here when you go," said the Doctor, giving the snail's shell a friendly pat.

The snail gently eased himself around and slid out of the surgery, shouting back a goodbye and giving a slight wiggle of his shell.

"I do wish snails would wait outside to be dealt with," said the Nurse as she cleaned the snail's slime trail from the floor before going home.

THE WASP'S STING

The wasp was buzzing around trying to find something to eat, going to and fro. A sudden breeze brought the smell of jam. An old jam jar had been thrown out from the house.

'That smells good,' he thought, quickly turning in the air and heading towards the smell.

As he turned sharply, something caught him in the back. He straight away thought he was being attacked, so he struck with the stinger in his tail.

Whatever was attacking him was strong – it threw him about all over the place. It felt like he was on a piece of string. When finally he became still he looked around to find that he had got caught in a net curtain on the washing line. He found that his stinger was entangled in the net curtain and he could not release it. So he wriggled and wriggled, and after a time he became free. But the stinger was beginning to hurt now.

Managing to fly very slowly, he settled on a large flower so he could have a rest and look at the damage to his stinger. One of the barbs was slightly bent and, worst of all, the stinger would not go back into the stinger pocket in his tail.

"Oh dear! I cannot fly with my stinger out – it is quite dangerous and it might break as well. I had better go and see Dr Earwig in his surgery now and get it seen to," he muttered to himself.

He flew straight to the surgery.

Dr Earwig heard the noise of the flying wasp a while before he came into the surgery.

The wasp entered the surgery walking very delicately because of the stinger being out all the time.

"I can see your trouble right away. How did you manage that?" Nurse Ant asked.

"I got caught in a net curtain, but the problem is now I cannot get my stinger to tuck away into my stinger pocket. It seems to be bent or catching on something," the wasp told the Doctor.

"Up on the stone slab with you and let's have a look at your stinger."

The Doctor and Nurse Ant helped the wasp on to the stone slab, and both of them could see straight away what was wrong. There were several little barbs on the stinger, and one of them had bent and was catching on the side of the pocket.

"Well, it's not good news, I'm afraid to say, Mr Wasp. We have got to take the bent barb off," the Doctor told the wasp.

"Will it hurt much?" asked the wasp.

"To be honest I'm not really sure. I've never

done any of these before, but I don't think it will. I think it will be like cutting a thick shell."

The Doctor went to a shelf on the wall and picked up a very sharp piece of flint.

"Now you must hold very still."

The Doctor started to cut the bent barb of the stinger. The first time the Doctor touched the barb with the flint the wasp flinched and closed his eyes.

"That did not hurt as much as I thought it would," said the wasp at last with a little tear in his eye.

The Doctor had finally managed to cut the barb away.

"Good! I hope it wasn't too painful for you," the Doctor said.

"It does feel sore," answered the wasp.

"I will now bathe it in nectar juice. This will clean it up and stop the germs getting in. Now, let us see you pull your stinger back into the pocket."

The wasp was still a little worried, but he slowly pulled the stinger back into the pocket. Unfortunately, where the missing barb was there was a small ragged bit still left on the stinger.

"Ouch! It has caught again," said the wasp.

"I'll have to smooth it down a little more."

The Doctor picked a little stone which had a very rough surface and began to smooth down the remains of the barb. After several minutes

the Doctor was satisfied that it would not catch any more.

"Try it now," the Doctor said.

"Wow, that's done it! Thank you, Doctor," the delighted wasp said.

The wasp then pushed the stinger in and out several times without thinking and Nurse Ant and Dr Earwig had to move out of the way of his tail.

"Go steady! If you catch us with that stinger of yours we will both need to see a doctor," shouted the Nurse.

"I'm very sorry," the embarrassed wasp said, and tucked his stinger into his stinger pocket so everyone was safe. "I had better go before I cause any more damage." With a grateful thank you the wasp went to the entrance and flew away.

"That was a near miss! I can't think where the other doctors are," said Nurse Ant to Dr Earwig.

THE FRIGHTENED CATERPILLAR

'My, my, these leaves are very scrumptious,' thought the caterpillar as he munched on the last leaf of the small flower stalk he was on. 'Nearly time to stretch on to the next flower. I'll just rest here in the shade for a while, and then I can get back to what I like best – eating nice juicy leaves.'

Without another thought about it, he lay down in the shade of another leaf and promptly went to sleep.

He had not been asleep long when he had a funny feeling of something tight about his tummy.

'Goodness me, I must have overeaten! That won't do. I really don't like having bellyache.'

He opened his eyes, and to his surprise he was not even on the leaf he had fallen asleep on; he was in the air, flying!

'What is happening to me?'

He looked around quickly, and he became very frightened indeed, because the tightness about his tummy was the beak of a big blackbird, which had scooped him off the leaf while he slept.

'What am I to do? I'm going to be eaten – just like I eat leaves.'

The blackbird was on her way to her nest to feed her chicks. The blackbird swooped down and landed on the edge of the nest. She dropped the caterpillar towards the beak of a little chick, but the chick missed the caterpillar. The caterpillar dropped between the twigs of the nest, into a little hole at the bottom of the nest where the chicks could not get through.

'I must lie still,' thought the frightened caterpillar, 'or they will see me moving and I will be eaten.'

The little caterpillar lay still for a long time – in fact, until all the birds had gone to sleep. By this time the little caterpillar, who had rolled into a ball so that he would not be noticed, was so scared and stiff that he could hardly unroll himself. After a while he was completely unrolled, but he was still very slow at moving. He did not want to disturb the birds in case they caught him again, so he quickly wormed his way through the bottom of the nest and on to the branch.

His tummy was now hurting badly, so he thought that a visit to the insect surgery, where he would get something for his sore tummy, was needed. The quickest way to get to the surgery was to follow a branch to its end and then get

on to the next tree and do the same there. So he went from tree to tree until he reached the tree next to the surgery.

After coming down the tree he walked a little through the grass and then he crawled under the shed. He was very sore indeed by now. The scratches on his tummy were hurting quite badly.

"Hello. What have you been up to? Your tummy looks sore and swollen – it's scratched very badly too. Would you like to come over here and sit yourself down so that Dr Earwig can have a proper look at you? He will not be long," Nurse Ant told him.

She left him to see what a little greenfly wanted who had just flown in.

Dr Earwig came to see the caterpillar a few minutes later. After a thorough look at the caterpillar's tummy, he told the caterpillar how lucky he was. "You have a nasty cut on your left side and deep scratches on your right, where the blackbird picked you up. We will put some nice healing ointment on it – this will take away the pain and it will get better very quickly."

The Doctor smothered the sides of the caterpillar with the ointment, which was made from honey and crushed strawberry leaves. The caterpillar wiggled and squirmed a little because the rubbing made the cuts and scratches hurt a little, but already the redness had faded and the swelling had gone down on both sides.

"Now, don't forget to come back to me if you still hurt in two or three days. Now go home and get some rest, but don't sleep out in the open or you might finish up as dinner for the blackbird family," said the Doctor as he went to see another patient.

"Bye-bye and thank you very much, Doctor and Nurse Ant, for your help," said the caterpillar as he walked painfully towards the door to make his way to the tree where he had been eating the leaves. I'm beginning to feel hungry again, so I'd better hurry before it gets dark.

A DAY'S WORK

Dr Earwig seemed to have three patients today. They were all waiting for his attention. Nurse Ant was getting them in order to see the Doctor.

"Who is the first patient, Nurse?" the Doctor asked.

"It is Mrs Glow-Worm with her baby," Nurse Ant said.

Mrs Glow-Worm had come to the Doctor with a tiny glow-worm baby wrapped in a leaf. He was moving about and seemed quite healthy.

"Good morning, Dr Earwig," Mrs Glow-Worm greeted the Doctor.

"This little chap seems to be full of energy," said the Doctor as he tickled the little bundle in the leaf carrier.

"That's the trouble – he is full of energy. He is not showing any signs of illness at all, but he does not seem to be able to glow. At this age my other two babies were glowing – not strongly, but quite well," stated Mrs Glow-Worm.

Dr Earwig examined the baby glow-worm

from top to bottom, but he could find no sign of illness. The Doctor was a little baffled, but he had an idea of what to do.

"Nurse Ant, can you help me, please?" asked the Doctor.

"Certainly. What do you want me to do?" she asked.

"I want you to cover me and the baby glow-worm with a large leaf so I can check his glow in the dark," instructed the Doctor.

Nurse Ant went outside and then returned with a large leaf.

"I'm ready now. Cover us up, then."

Under the leaf the Doctor strained his eyes, but still he could not see the baby glow-worm's glow. He was just about to give up when the little worm sneezed and there, just for a moment, was a little flicker of light, and then it faded. The Doctor was pleased. He uncovered himself and the baby glow-worm.

"Not to worry, Mrs Glow-Worm – this baby is not as strong as your other two were at this age. You see, just now when the baby glow-worm sneezed the effort of sneezing made him glow just a little. So give him another week, get him to eat more dandelion leaves and I'm sure he will be OK. If not, bring him back to me next week, please."

"Thank you, Doctor," Mrs Glow-Worm said gratefully, and picking up the baby glow-worm she went out of the surgery.

Next to see the Doctor was a big wood ant, limping badly.

"Now, what have you done?" asked the Doctor, glancing at the injured leg.

"We were burrowing down, making a new tunnel, when a heavy stone fell across my foot. And it hurts," the wood ant told him.

"Oh dear! It's quite badly scraped and there is a big bruise starting to show. Other than that, I don't think there is any serious damage. I'll get Nurse to give you some rose-petal ointment. Now, rub this on three times a day and you will be digging tunnels again in no time."

"Thanks, Doctor," the wood ant said as he limped from the surgery with a few oohs and aahs.

Nurse Ant came to the Doctor with a big slug following her.

"I'm afraid, Doctor, Master Slug here has been caught out in the sun and has got sunburnt."

"Dear dear, let me have a look at your back – yes, it looks very sore in places. I think we will cover it with some nectar juice to stop it blistering. Once it is dry we will cover your back with a dry leaf. This will protect you from the sun, so you will not be burnt again. But I really think you should go home in the dark – it will be a lot cooler then."

"That's a good idea. I'm not in any hurry anyway," said the slug.

So they all sat around chatting until it was time for the slug to go.

"It's nearly dark, so I think I'll be off home now," said the slug, looking out of the surgery door.

"Yes, I would say it was a good time to go. Goodnight and mind how you go," Dr Earwig said.

"Well, I'm on my way home now. I have put everything away. I'll see you in the morning," Nurse Ant said as she was going out of the surgery.

"That's fine and thank you," the Doctor shouted as the Nurse disappeared out of the door.